PIMP SUASION

PRESENTS

WHITE DWARF

The Priest

Not Just Alphabets Publishing

In Association with The Priest LLC

Fort Worth, Texas

ISBN 13: 978-1-7338810-1-2

First Trade Paperback Printing March 2019

Printed in the U. S. A.

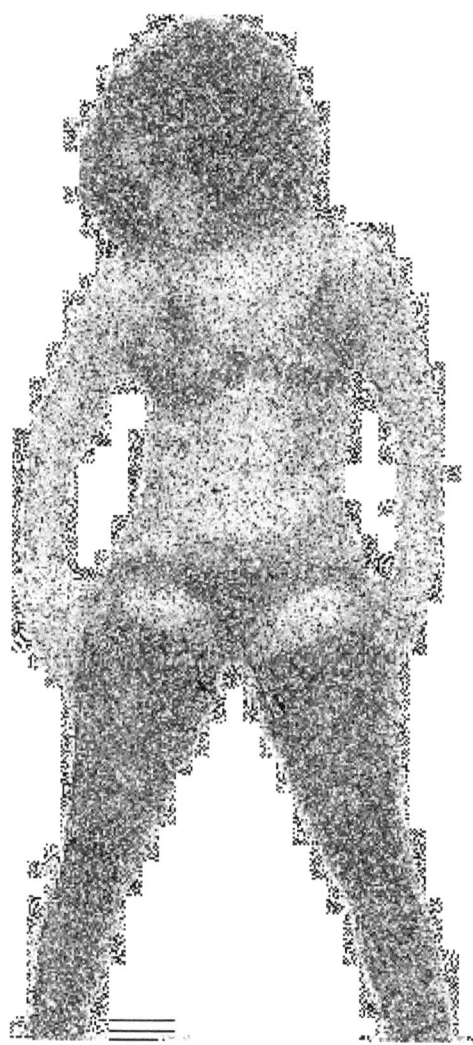

Introduction

In this book many of the subjects discussed are looked down upon, it is my intent to speak in their defense because of my position in the game. In which Persuasion brings us to Pimpin and also brings us to white collar words such as "White Slavery". Even though the practice of slavery would have only proliferated after the invention of agriculture during the Neolithic Revolution about 11,000 years ago. The earliest known records of slavery is treated as an established institution.

So we find through the years it is not prison we are afraid of, it's coming hand to hand with Revenge or should I say insight and intelligence allowing us to flip the script. My purpose is not for the strong but making the hesitant chase their weakness. Your weakness will always be your own Demons. So, always kill the devil quick while you have him.

I was taught to think on your feet and move with the moments, knowing we hang on a tire rope and must find balance. Life is like the streets we drive on. We all start off in the same lane but we all turn towards different destinations. This revelation is why I was created. If you have an imagination you can imagine the consequence of your own actions, seeing there are no physical only mental repercussions. Bringing you to the nature of "Pimpin". It takes discipline because intellect is the future and manners make a man. So you can either live in the streets as a peasant or a boss.

Although you have to prove your loyalty, how can you be proven loyal when you can't be proven faithful? Providing that men are innocent to the incident not necessarily undeserving of the crown. We should hate the sin not the sinner. A fact for my closest people I will kill be cause of you not for you.

In conclusion I would like to be awake when everyone else is sleep, when my death bed has come to me my haters will be awakened to keep my mama alive.

Rest In Peace

Papa Johnny Chatman - Grandma Margret Chatman

To: Lil Wilbert - Black Men Killed by Police

Lil Peter - T. Bone - Grandma Essie Galmore

all the fallen soldiers

Funny Face - Free Dev - Free Buddy

Free Pat - Free Carly - Free Dez - Free Lil E

Dedicated To The Struggle

The Street Scholar

Pimp Suasion

Presents: White Dwarf

The Street Scholar

16.9.13.16   19.21.1.19.   9.15.14

Table of Contents:

White Dwarf

a small very "dense" whitish star of low "luminosity"

Simplified - a small very "dull" whitish star of low "clearness or light"

I chose the title 'White Dwarf' because we all lose our way, sometimes our goals are in sight but are not seen because we have unreasonable intentions. Most of the time it seems we are the Diamonds in the Rubble and all we need to do is be discovered. Although waiting on someone else to discover our greatness, leaves us in our best interest to try and discover self. There are moments in life we expect or except what and how we do things, but we don't except who we are or even care to explore.

I wrote this book using reflective thoughts and experiences, not to protest to the world of what I can do but to make the "dull" shine and the "low luminosity" of things or myself show up brighter. I am here to show you what training your mind and feelings can produce. Most importantly the thoughts are to make my mother proud of me and show her that we came from the mud and now it ain't a stain on me. That caging yourself before any one else does; can breed a wide range of proficiency on you or your terms instead of waiting on others terms. Though now on others terms, "I am caged", I've shined brighter in this least amount of time; than the unknown amount of time it would have taken for me to lock myself away in my own cage. So these are my reflective thoughts that brought about "White Dwarf"

Special Thanks

To my mother who has been my spiritual, mental and physical backbone. To Dominique Park who helped me start and finish this process. To Britany Stafford who undying love inspired and motivated my essence. And to my children who lived through the struggle until we rose from the pain. Thanks to the elders who showed us the way.

money was the motive;
dreams was the Reason...

Candy Drop

1

Pimp Suasion

#1

Pimp Persuasion

The greatness of pimpin is mostly about the money, but evenly about his pimpin as a whole that point to his guidance and intelligence, bringing formation and function to the body. Most who don't know, think that as the head or the author of anything you are out to search for its contents; but the wisdom to create and preserve is already installed. The head is only obtaining the beauty in those contents, because we all know everything is not beautiful at first sight and everything and everyone has beauty in them.

Pimpin is only planting the seeds and nurturing them to their specific growth and that exhibits the wisdom you possess. So in breeding and growing of the seeds planted, it shows the infinite intelligence that was built from mentally in you to the physical of you. I have looked at so much of the ancient errs and they are far more beautiful then the new age arts, so in art as in pimpin, author, or master I find beauty is more beyond the surface. It's something about the inside of beauty that makes it more complex as if they have been aged to the extremities of a fruit that has to become ripe.

Pimp as the creator must find the secrets of beauty and create everything he comes across from that recipe. And that recipe must be evident of everyone or things particular task. In its entirety a pimp must remind its creation of the need to appreciate him. Most will try to make sense of their suffering that you meet, but your objective is to make them feel your coming into their life is something of precise gain. Though some will appear or even be very ungrateful and unappreciative. You have to show them your intelligence by listing the experience suffered without your hedge of protection to open there eyes. Understand some will choose without sight and some will accept your greatness but not cherish it and that's cool as long as they respect and pay.

Most will quickly understand your meaning and their purpose and humbly acknowledge your intelligence and presence becoming grateful of it. This is all of excepting where you've been to control the new and envision great purpose by facilitating it to your followers. You must make them in some way feel their contribution is huge, because " like ants are a people not strong, yet they prepare food for the summer; the locust have no king yet they all advance in rank." Now even though a pimp doesn't operate out of or in emotions, your women will experience emotions through the lessons and orders you teach or make, so you must be on point like a needleless dick at all times.

That is why everybody is not made for this because most people are more physical than mental, more mental than physical, but this is all mental ending up a mental work out. Even though all persons are unique and different. All are built the same or upon the same common wisdom and intelligence, because all seek happiness and all experience tears or sadness. So when you think of the possibilities of manipulating anyone, determine their response to problem solving and it's all downhill after that. Because in the problem solving it shows there intelligence in hard work, but the body will present eloquence and promote them more supreme. Then and only then can you use that against them as an example that one cannot work without the other premeasuring them to ask you how they can make themselves whole and everything comes in agreement with self.

I estimate 10% of the time you can approach a

women as "pimpin" I think it is because of your understanding and knowing their character and or potential. The other 90% of the time you should let them choose, their knowing how you walk, talk, and define yourself will tune them into what you possess and sometimes when these ho's come in a pimp presence for some reason they don't even know why they are there. So it's your moment to give them reason to be there and stay there.

The eye presents an immaculate example of irreducible complexity, but it will make you look of the prideful. Understand that pimpin is a masterpiece of conception and execution. The trauma lies in the emotions; "for even the strongest can be bent and broken", so understand that. A lot of the times pride can prevent us from receiving the whole concept of everything. A pimp is more like the skin to the body and to his bitches he is the shield. When you bring together all of the parts; your plan is to make sure all the pieces to the puzzle are present, because therefore it will engage in the absence of other pieces to the puzzle. Also, make sure your instructions are never in conflict because then it will present trauma and a powerful test to the pimp, skin, author; shield of protection. Know that a pimp uses all his bitches, but is conservative on how he uses his resources and never uses more than one when only one will suffice. Know that the body depends on you as the head, but the system is dependent on intelligence, vigilance and vigor.

It is easier to direct a ho, when she knows that from the time of conception humans have been under attack. So go through it because it is inevitable between you, your bottom bitch, and so on down the chain of interactions within or between levels are hugely complex. Make sure there is no other way of looking at you and them not experience a glimpse of pimpin as wisdom within. It is important to know spitting game is not always the thing that captures something. Most of the time it's the conversation and it operates the same way each time the individual is exposed and they will respond to each individual with exactly the same speed and intensity.

When you pressure something or someone you find fertilized fields in which your objective is to be productive rapidly. Making your bitches tough is a major factor, because then they lose the ability to recognize themselves. Know their response become damage accomplishment of very difficult task of their outcome or overcome. Through your mastery they will seek the definition of your maturity. Know that through ruthless pursuits, some will try and grow outside of the body, all will have their points of total or occasional weakness and will want to come running back. At this point you must let them go don't chase them.

With clear eyes we must observe the massive accomplishments of the intricate and sophisticated from the moment of development, because survival and hope is meaningless if a pimp's intelligence isn't expressed through the entire body. Make them believe that being supplied with emotional experience keeps their eyes open and the heart racing in excitement. Therefore when your seeds are growing a foundation, it shows the beautiful mind of the pimp or author.

Pimpin 101

A.

"Know that a pimp uses all his bitches, but is conservative on how he uses his resources and never uses more than one when only one will suffice."

- The Priest-

Power In The Moment

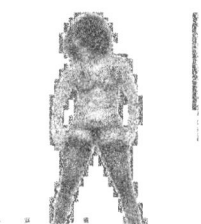

#2

Philosophy / Pimp Satisfied

#2

Philosophy / Pimp Satisfied

A philosopher is simply a man of theory, which is based on hypothesizing as in meaning an educational guess. Though some say a guess is simply a guess. Its not because that person is down in the darkness never wanting to understand the light but the facts others are down in the light rooted with a strong foundation to build on. Therefore you must be a "scholar" or a learned person and seek all of the knowledge around you whether good or bad. Take what is unnecessary from it and leave what supports the all-around picture of things. Therefore when you began to ponder about them, your mentality regress those things and your mind becomes your memory card vision.

So the ideas of subjects all around in which interest us are obtained and help us advance as "reflective thinkers." Plus this allow us to inhabit the things which have been our downfall or pleasure, even greatness and we become persons whose philosophical perspective makes it possible to meet trouble calmly, actually there is no other way but to see the beauty of a philosophical being; the sum of ideas and convictions of an individual life. Meanwhile I think it's the reason that some of our professions become something of "theology" which is the study of religious faith, practice, and experience, because we study them like we examine our religious faith. We practice it for perfection, but the experience in a whole make up superior to our cause. This leads my respect of and for the pimp and pimpin. Most people think a pimp and pimpin is the same thing, its not.

"Pimp" expresses a noun, which is the word that is the name of a subject of discourse (as a person or place). Though pimpin is the expression of a verb, which is a word that is the grammatical center of a "predict" and expresses an act, occurrence, or mode of being, so in religion the "pimp" represents the "pulpit" which signifies the ordinances of which is establish within that thing. Therefore" pimpin" represents the pasturing of, which examples his intellect, his prestige, his leadership, his stand, his reverence, or his loyalty. In which pimpin and pasturing, they articulate (able to speak; expressing one's self readily and effectively) to their ho's / congregation, guiding them to their team / alter, in search of progression / obliverance.

Though the word that stuck out to me in "pimpin" being a verb is predicate because it's the part of a sentence or clause that expresses what is said of the subject. So that's special to me because anything that is spoken should be spoken whole hearted never half, because anything that is worth speaking on and representing should be made clear and affectionate to the crowd or who is being receptive. Plus that's the only time you should release your emotions; being when your performing, cause this is where your money comes from, so therefore the "pimp" becomes the religious artifact, while pimping becomes the religious commandment studied and expresses in act to symbolize its purpose.

Which leads me to pimps satisfied, but before I start the pimps not accountable for your assumptions, he or she is only accountable for their actions just like anyone else. Assumption also lead you to think that these ho's are eager to pleasure their pimp because of abuse, weakness, control, and there undying love. Even though that plays a factor, it's deeper than that though. That's only the shell you have to break, because you have to cook the yoke to understand the essence of this pimpin that your swallowing; she does these things for her pimps satisfied look, but rarely received it and not knowing she's really searching for "own" satisfaction, to say she put him on the top or made him smile, so she searches for simple expression.

A real pimp isn't moved by the money she brings, goals, or accomplishments, even if sometimes he should (lol), he is only moved by the point of her willingness to please and then she is necessity. But to her his face is emotionless, thoughtless, unsatisfying and yet pleasure at the same time. A lot of us unknowingly think that to satisfy is to be 100% but it's not. Satisfied only means to make happy, pay what is due, to meet requirements, or contentment" to ease the mind." So in meaning to satisfy her pimp is only temporary and then process is an ongoing state of mind, practically saying. She should never feel she has done enough, because her job is to ho knowing sex sells and it has been that way for centuries and want ever stop, so get this money.

To satisfy is like appetite; you're hungry, you eat, and get full, but you always end up hungry again; though in pimpin your always hungry, because your hands and pockets are like endless pits. A top notch bitch gets the most not the lesser, what "pimp C" said. Though a true pimp with charisma never shows if he's receiving the most or the lesser he leaves bickering to the assumption makers and that builds his legacy. Also some think charisma and flamboyant is the same and its not. Charisma is a personal quality of leadership arousing popular loyalty or enthusiasm. Flamboyant is marked by or given to strikingly elaborate or colorful display or behavior, in other words a clown. Anyways live to soak up the game; don't live to get soaked up in the game.

My Parachute was useless
so I dove off the cliff
of Contemplation...

- Bad Bitch Status -

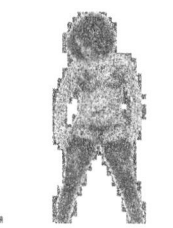

#3

Pimpin My Growth of Mentality
Through Sacrificing the Physical

#3

Pimpin My Growth of Mentality
Through Sacrificing the Physical

What is it? As I sit contemplating of what am I missing or what do I not get. While waiting for a break through or blessing we only think sometimes that everything will come in due time, but maybe it's something we have not presented, something is absent, or a moment that hasn't been captured. Man I wreck my brain for about an hour and I'm still not sure if this is the reason but I came up with this profound little chapter. And this is about Tommy Chatman vs. Pimp Suasion, darkness and light, left and right, or better yet revenge vs. business.

You see my mentality at this moment is so right; I can't go left! And my physical is so left it refuses to go right! Therefore leaving my life seeming or feeling orthodox, because everyone has a good vs. evil fight, right! But this is acknowledged vs. knowledge. I acknowledge my circumstances were worth seeing, observing, and conquering, but the knowledge will come in conflict with those circumstances that will leave my cotton stained. I say that, saying that we are all to evolve into better or greater constantly, but by change we are never to forget where we come from to remain who we are. But sometimes remembering or being reminded of those circumstances will cause much "havoc."

Even though a man /women smile and remain of composure or in a complex state, doesn't mean life is fair. It only means life has made him sacred to eviscerate the troubles they bestow on them. Meanwhile we are left with demands that no one couldn't even begin to speak of and I could never expose to you. I am the epitome of the end of toleration, yet I am also the euphony creating a major production birthing a harvest of leverage. How and why did I get here though? I understand that my alter egos were collected and at the right moment present themselves, but as everyone or thing it leaves one fighter to gain superiority. Therefore with everything being collective along the way, I have been in constant conflict with the old and the new.

That being because as the old I can be your nightmare if activated, but as new I am unpredictable. Old I was physical and mental evenly. Now I am all mental therefore new and old together pronounced me as a glacier, but apart they promote me as perfection of chaos. What part of this am I supposed to get and will it release me being Tommy Chatman the savage or Pimp Suasion voice similar to a wand of magic. I lose Tommy, my mother loses the child of remorse; if I lose the pimp, and then my family loses its legacy I bring. So do I sacrifice my tears and struggle or history? Tears and struggles made us stronger for the fight and history rewards us for that fight. Actually writing this I don't even understand what language I'm speaking. When I make my decision will I be able to restore mind to its full capacity? Canceling one the other might or might not at first, but sooner or later will leave a void somewhere or somehow. Evolving from Tommy, struggle, sacrifice, hard times, plus the street life I never thought that by becoming "pimp" could show beauty in the beast. Mainly because Louisiana breeds beast and its harshness doesn't disperse the beauties only the jungle.

I guess the real question is if I'm willing to leave the jungle or the Garden of Eden and it seems simple, but is so energetic. Tommy is tired of the old, the same, the ordinary, and the cycle. While the pimp is energetic about his visions, betterment, his wholeness, open eyes, and his unawareness but gaining of finer things. Superior has become an understatement to his mentality. But then you also have to ask yourself, is it the faith in my pimpin or is it that misery provided these strategies of a god to remain in my company. So how do I deliver myself from the anger to sanity or Tommy to pimp. Tommy was created by loyalty, but people and life has fallen to be loyal. The pimp is lonely and pimpin has brought great satisfaction to his position in life.

Therefore the old me is dead and gone, now the new me is raising hell to show the world what they've created. Even though we say we know, we really have no idea on how to finalize victory in this situation. So the best thing is to drive to the finish line and victory greets whichever side it greets, just stay in preparation for the choice. To be dedicated to my mentality, sacrifice and physical does that bring death, because everyone that makes a choice betrays something or someone. A lot of times I wonder did my ambition turn me envious, was it what I seen, did, and heard that made me who and what I became numbing me of my emotions?

Did the of life penitentiary rehabilitate me or surrender me to the conflict of past and present. Better yet does becoming a scholar lead me blind to fall in the ditch? Because the reflective thinker at some moments become blind to the physical thinker. Plus does the man in the mirror only reflect the things he has devoured? Because if so no matter whom I do or don't become I will always see both. Therefore my worries are not life and death, but will I seek destiny or revenge. Shit fuck it Tommy's gone with the old and pimp is here with the new. So relax and simmer down pimipin.

Decision is only a temporary contraction to the bigger picture.

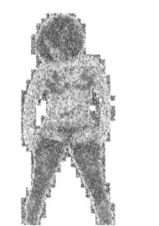

#4

Appetite

#4

Appetite

You know the craziest thing came to me today and it was appetite. It's not as much that we lust for things, but more that we crave for things. And I say crave because a lot of the things we want need or we require, though it isn't till we can't have it or it seems to far fetch to receive that we lust for. But appetite is a little of both, because you can have it and want more or you can never have been in grips of that thing and you still have an appetite for it. Matter of fact your appetite gets stronger.

To me it's not ambition, drive, the need to hope, or will. It is because we chase a mental and physical tastes that we've come across or we've applauded its presence. If money is the root of all evil then appetite is its parents. If success is everything hoped for appetite is its faith. If karma is a bitch then appetite is her navigation. If love hurts then appetite is that two edge sword. If blood sweat and tears are how we earn our strips, then appetite is the master and we are its slaves.

When most people say they have appetite we mostly think of hunger in general, but it's actually a liking for something specific; a choice. We as American people we are very picky in everything. "Aperture" is French for to strive after, and "peters" is French for to go. So to simply say a word that we use in association with our food has a deeper meaning when everything comes together or it falls through the wire. In which to strive after means to labor hard for, but when we use appetite in our interest it seems that it is a natural process becoming effortless. So if appetite is indeed what is said here, does that mean that even the surest and most luciest people in the world possess this strive. That in deed they are simply putting on a show of helplessness.

Does this means that appetite allowing us to know what we want, give us possession over functioning people? Does it make us certain in the state or condition we're in? Does it allow us to endure for something that is temporary? Is it really the things we want and need; is it really appetite that made Cain kill Abel, or a mother kill her husband for insurance money? Is appetite the cause of war or betrayal?

Is it appetite what makes us show favor for something wanted or needed? Are is it appetite that makes us hate or want the words of denial or approval? Was it rebellion or appetite that made me, so encouraged to learn the streets? You here some people speak as if they have lost all hope, but is it because really their appetite is begging them to give up or surrender? Does this mean that deep down inside that everybody's fulfillment will never be, especially for the successful as well as the non-successful?

Does this insinuate that everyone has a endless pit deep down inside of them, that we haven't discovered and probably will still never give recognition to. Now that we have gained insight and we are not blind to ourselves, will we rather still have a blind fold on us? Therefore does appetite allow us to sacrifice the process of knowing and not knowing? Is it appetite that encourages us that new is better than old, but then uses it to its discretion? Probably so and then probably not, but I just want us to know that appetite is deeper then hunger or desire it's more of that then Adam, Eve, and the serpent. We want all we have, but we also want what we can't have.

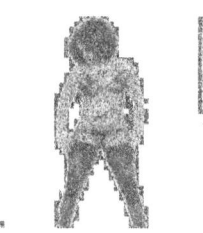

#5

Pen and Paper

#5

Pen and Paper

To most the pen and paper is of no importance or even needed, only a necessity. To the great in which can only express their life, emotion, progression, or meaning it is faith in everything hoped for. Though really I see the pen and paper as the apparition of time, past and present." The pen represents my veins that bleed through struggle and the paper represents my heart, which pumps for motive." In this recognition, the pen represents me in a way that is unknown, but surprisingly precious. Sometimes it seems as if when my mind wonders, my pen hypothesis, and then paper gathers everything to conclusion.

I have witnessed the best and the worst, vision the least and the greatest coming to grips with a lot of understanding. Pen and paper still means to me though as a heaven that can't be replaced. For years starting when I was only 7 years of age, I jotted down things unknowing to my knowledge. I stared at a tablet until I had something to say without recognition of what it would become. Throughout those years focus and ambition gave me a variety of pure substances. So now every time I have the pen and paper joined in holy matrimony. I feel like a new born in mother and fathers hand of safety, but who am I to write of this without a university or college degree.? Nobody! But then Bill Gates didn't even finish school and he went on to make millions if not billions. Though his standards and accomplishments does not stand far from me, I just stand for mind of theory or reflection that can completely exhausted through pen and paper.

Where am I to go from here 99.9% has me dubious of my conquest. Regardless of life's ill's, everything becomes of a standstill or paralyzed. When the pen makes love with the paper and stimulates my legacy. People say that every men and women must cry and it's true because I have shed one or two tears, but my emotions are not of the human kind. This presents moral thoughts; moral have been written ages ago, but today morals are only spoken and branched off of. So therefore we come up with agreements in writing to obviate the loss of business in our morals. Even though the pen and pad is both used for truth and of being fallacious, we can never be false unless proven.

If this is examined, the pen and paper to every one of its use normally are more comfortable in providing their character in it; which allows writing majority to be of truth and less of fallacious. In that being said things can either be true or false never both as a whole. Either truth misleading to false or false fully misleading to the truth .Through history things have been written and unaware that they would leave questions and deep thought, but what was the point of pen and paper to leave curiosity in the cat of tomorrow. I will be unsatisfied even if my pen is recognized and my paper not is framed in glass, because the whole tree or plastic didn't receive that same appreciation. The pen and paper has told some of the best and worst stories calculated and declined but still it has never been given proper nurturing.

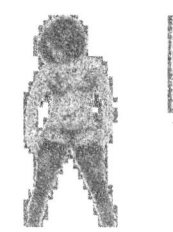

#6

World In 3rd Person

#6

World In 3rd Person

Why and how do I see the world in third person? As if I can't be in it, surrounded by it, together with it, forever associated, or vindictive to it. Sometimes I see the pleasure in it and hope for my own acceptance to it, but more often I see the ugliest parts and live or play it from afar. One reason is that I'm so upset as I sit back and watch people so irresponsible to achievement. That so many of us respect being unchangeable. Is it that when they make excuses, we elaborate there excuses unconsciously and help them except settling.

At times it seems that the history of fighters have fought in a long hard struggle, only in the present day to be defeated. Sometimes it seem that even though we call ourselves winners that true victory is farfetched. Now that I have become stronger in mind, I go through a lot more than physical could ever take me through. Though I am grateful, I am also saddened by the things I see. In the physical it seemed that the world was maintaining. Now in the mental and stepping back observing things, I find that we are lost and headed to no other destination but our own destruction.

They say let the world and the people in it be what and who they are, but a harden heart has no choice but to soften because it isn't easy to see a whole world vanish right before your eyes. In which as a pimp I'm not supposed to, but I can't help but to want to put that "s" on my chest. Therefore life as a whole has left us as a game of chess and we have returned to simply play a game of checkers. I wonder does it start off from our pointless and simple minded conversations!! Or the division and combination of race. Or the fact that we still grade one gender less than the other!!

Looking at the world it seems that there are no more stepping stones; only crumbs from the bread and we still fail to surpass them. When I was young I seen the o.g's (original gangsta's) but now I see clowns .Maybe there are no more teachers only students and no more guidance means no more progression. We went from refusing to give in, to refusing to hold on in the struggle. Though I am proud to say that at least the younger who are misled are eager to walk for the old righteous cause. Discipline is no more and renegades have taken place. We think of "if's" as statements of the past , but if we use them in extent to the present we may be able to birth a change of our direction .

I love her more now though because she has left me to my thoughts and written me to my legacy. I cannot rush the inevitable, I can only coach you through the process. "Time keeps slipping because we have lost our grips of history." *I GUESS AT THE END OF THINGS WE ONLY THINK ABOUT THE BEGINNING...*

Paying Homage

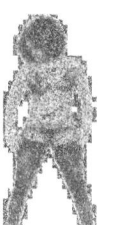

#7

Tired

#7

Tired

At some time or point; you get tired of being tired, tired of being patient. You can hold so much that you learn to expose just a little. A heart of gold, a mind of status, but a body in agony. I live therefore I must keep moving. This is not depression this is chance to soar or drown. I am a critic of price, of position, of sacrifice, of fear, and fate. What is there to see? What is there to know? What is there to examine? Why should I thrive? To hell with questions, because majority of them even past the day of death will go unanswered. I must keep searching, keep pondering, keep walking and keep escaping the breath of giving up. At times instead of holding up my words or posting them together, it feels I'm holding up the walls of china. That I'm running under two miles of water. That I'm singing my heart out to a voiceless song.

Is there time to rejuvenate? Is there a moment of approach? I want so bad to walk that thin line that everyone refuses to walk, but it is invisible to a tired soul. I am here to stay, but it seems that I have already failed in staying here. You as the pimp is strong in every way, but that has become my poison. My morning has turned from clay to marble at times; then from gold to dust… It seems that when you're never meaning for things to happen, they happen with meaning. I don't engulf the day of desolation, but there is a time when mensuration is the inevitable. Understand that I may bounce around on this subject because I'm tired of the guidelines or staying in bounds. At times I've become weak to living in discretion, because terms have made me blind.

What if energy is a gamble of survival? As a man I support the front line but it seems that when it's showdown I'm here alone. Tired of regarding to sanity when there isn't even any composer to be kept. A foot away from the touchdown, but all I find is first base on a baseball field. Caught up in the matrix, how must I find completion to my any one thing? Abating seems to be easy entangled in affliction, but mustn't we succeed at something? I was hungry until I ate , I was blind until I opened my eyes , it was your lesson until it was mine, and I was tired until I slept . I am here and yet I can still stand.

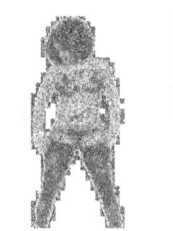

#8

It Was Yours Til It Was Mine

#8

It Was Yours Til It Was Mine

I have seen your mind drifting so distorted and yet practical. It was yours until it was mine. Humiliation covered your face as the cherry dipped in chocolate discouraged and disgraced, but it was yours til it was mine. Have you ever dreamed or possessed the happiest tears? And yes I've waited in the stars and wondered if you would accompany me here. Satisfied with the clouds, it was yours til it was mine.

What is your desire as I give them to your weakness? Let me listen to your heart beat, as I operate on your priceless worth. Take my hand as we journey through the hemisphere of retribution. I am your captain, your leader, your oppressor, your king, and empire state of mentality. Though it was yours til it was mine. Take a trip or vacancy from self, let me train your emotions and upgrade your illusions of exclusive knowledge because success it was yours til it was mine.

I am the truth, you are the light, and we together become inscription that can never be over thrown. In time there will be nothing smoother, nothing more essential, and nothing that can be more compatible. Though it was only yours til it was mine. Here I stand grounded in this pimpin, excluded from the un pristine of yesterday. Later I will crack your egg and wipe the yolk from your eyes as the warmth of your harmony becomes preponderant. Life was yours til it was mine caught up in it's volatile being victimized.

Sometimes it seem there's never a right time to begin , but for now focus on ending the old therefore making our way up beginnings hill knowing and understanding that it was yours til it was mine. Baptized in my protection, but to the world you will be drenched in stigma. Paralyzed in reflection, it was yours until it was mine. It was grace before it could breathe, so you were laced before you were conceived. Pledged to submit injunction, denial will only cage in the will, because it was yours til it was mine.

I heard you speaking of an angel, though when I came you cried wolf. I see your vision because it was mine before it was your .How can you live without the quanda-ry, because I have bathed in its absolution. I must compli-ment your beautiful meaning, because therefore or some-how it seems it was mine before it was yours .Before I knew how to respond to precious, you presented yourself to me. But giving to the abyss and taken by zest. Incom-pleteness tires only the objection to greatness, you found that which is not in self, is in me humbly accepting that it was mine until it was yours. If I be lifted then you can't be turned down. A story could be told, but the game could only be sold. A lie is easy because its cause, but our truth can only survive as detrimental because of its affect. It was yours only til it was mine.

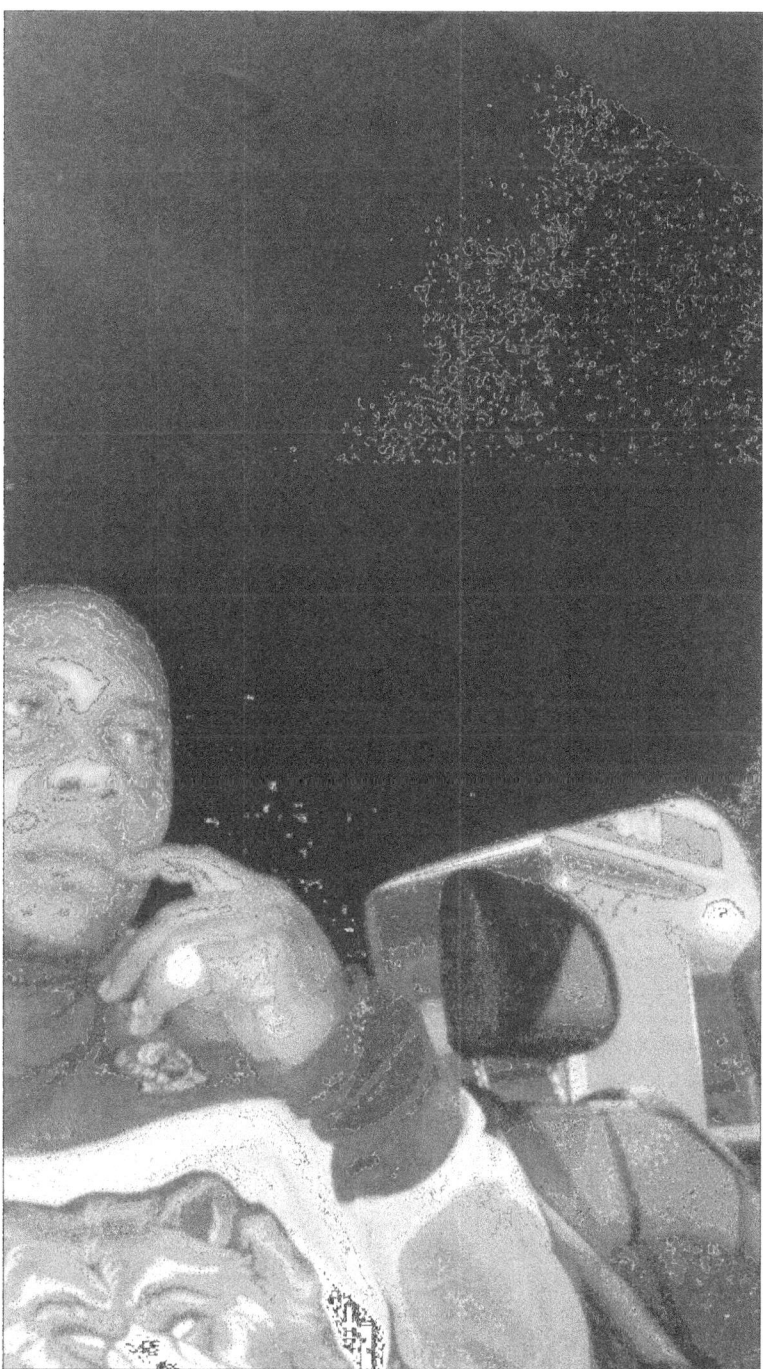

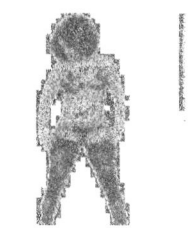

#9

A Crown So Heavy

#9

A Crown So Heavy

The top is so close to the bottom, yet the bottom is so far from the top. This comes about because it's so hard to reach the top, but so easy to fall to the bottom. To receive my crown I had to take so much, so to lose my crown I would have to give so much. To have a crown is so great, but to keep a crown is forever a burden because the top is only a seat and the bottom is it's pedestal .In which even though greed make some ignorant to the fact, it is always clear who sits at the top but at the bottom you can't always be or make sure of the steps you make; there's so many traps and unseen puppeteers. At times, a life as a searching peasant is way more acceptable to me than being of monition (cautious) crown holder.

I have been at the bottom which has exposed me to so many countless options, but here at the top I've only seen countless scams. The crown is not made heavy by simply just the job itself, but by the job contradicting duties. At the bottom there is only sacrifices, but at the top there is only eliminations. In which things or people around your throne become equivalent with the women we sneak out to or with, but when you greet her your response "I'm here to address you not undress you. "It takes her perception of things. Therefore under a held crown , there lies deception, manipulation, greed, ambition, murder, war, backstabbing, schemes for bigger pictures, less and less morals, vision, mastery, no emotions and loneliness etc… The crown holder does not possess all these traits, but he is surrounded by them and baptized in them so he might as well possess them. Due to the crown we hold the end result is not the bottom but death, because everyone see how at the top you are; so when you fall their afraid you might regain composure and come for it again. So remember I told you that it's elimination on an "I'll let him make it type scale but only this time. The heartless can never miss a beat when there playin the tempo" (P.S)

I think the crown is wore on the head because that's where its role or position is carried out: the head or the brain. A crown is flamboyant in the physical, but is a million tons on the mental. Having a crown is worse than fighting 10 hyenas, 30 tigers and 80 leopards because at least there you know who wins. Though with the crown you only know who's winning for the moment. And it's crazy because a crown represents order, royal, victory, and the hardest part 'but any cheap shot made or giving by friends or enemies of no loyalty, bring the meaning of your crown to a disaster.

    You see ½ of an inch to lost discretion can leave the best or the greatest laying in shame. "a crown so heavy or so heavy a crown, is like me wishing upon a star and the star just laying on my wish. The crown brings toleration to its lowest worth; nothing. My crown, if I take it off when I sleep at night, it want be there in the morning. If I leave it on as I sleep at night, my head want be there in the morning. All cause a crown so heavy want allow me to float back to the bottom , only swim with the fishes.

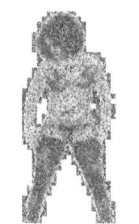

#10

The Missing Link

#10

The Missing Link

Thoreau, Gandhi, and Mandela wanted us to know that we live in an era right now, that we can reinvent ourselves when we choose. Plus instead of keeping the original reasons of greatness, we recast the wisdom of the great thinkers in the shape of a great illusion. So therefore we blame the past thinkers `for our misconception, blindness, or stupidity of morals. When really we should be blaming ourselves for the delusion we brought in and lead to the fall of our morals. Everybody say that the original thinkers are missing from today, but all that statement does is provide us with the excuses to fail.

We are the missing links because we want step up, sacrifice, or even observe what's going on. There's the ancient creators, the progressors of time; but instead our progression has declined. We figured that the struggle was too much, because we're innovators we don't have to live by the original things, and that time is not important to our careless ways or position. So that kept us holding, going from being diluted a little, to being weak, and becoming the missing link. This has giving us hopelessness in success and our future, but fuck us right? What about the children? How do we change or get back to making history worth learning about? Not the pursuit of happiness , because that only left us chasing pleasure .But the pursuit of dreams , because either way pure or diluted leaves progressors of many things and ways. It brings back the possibilities instead of everyone chasing the guarantees.

Walden states that, "I learned this , at least , by my experiment :that if one advances confidently in the direction of his dreams , and endeavors to live which he has imagined , he will meet with success unexpected in common hours ."I can say that we haven't began to walk ,crawl ,pace, and far from running toward giving hope to our future .We tell our kids that they can become what they want , but than one hour later we tell them" life's a bitch and shoot for what you can see." We are pitiful and hypocrites. I might sound like an ancient warrior but rise up and take a stand .Gandhi says: "If we could change ourselves, the tendencies in the world would also change. As a man changes his own nature , so does the attitude of the world change towards him. We need not wait to see what others do. "Today's society is caught on or with trend, if it isn't popular it isn't acknowledged!

"When my homeboy's sleep I cannot sleep; he has just ended his day and I have just begun." (Pimp Suasion) and that's crazy because we're quick to leave things unaccomplished, to seem accomplished with the rest. Therefore setting a trend of being accepted. Being the missing link is worse than being the weakest link, because you can strengthen the weak but 98% of the time we never find the missing and when we do it's never good or great results. Mandela in 1994's inaugural address states that, (our deepest fear) "it is not that we are inadequate. Our deepest fear is that we are powerful beyond measure. It is our light, not our darkness, that most frightens us .

We are ourselves, who am I to be brilliant, gorgeous, talented, fabulous? Actually, who are you not to be? You are a child of God. Your playing small does not serve the world... As we are liberated from, our presence automatically liberates others. "We have taken the context of coming to the light, for coming out of the closet. We have taken change to forgetting where we come from. So the disgrace that the weak has given, supplied the ones who can stand with the refusing to stand. We have the right to imagine, give effort and be disciplined and persistent. Do not give in to the oppressors, give out with the progression and we'll no longer be the **missing link.**

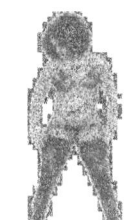

#11

Contemplated Time

#11

Contemplated Time

Is there a heaven for a "Gee" for his mentality of greatness, contemplated so mentally. Looking through minutes I find hours, but in hours I find that years have been invested to my accommodations. My steps were ordered by my city of gold, because it is not steps of direction but lyrics of strategy. I come from a world where you only eat what you can catch, a world where slippers are worn not survivors and a world of manipulated rules. Walk with me and I can show you life, put your face low to the earth and listen to the nature, and fall unconscious to its experience the illusion of contemplated time and motion of her stroke. Time should feel and be like the first hit of marijuana; smooth, and sacred or like sippin that activist; powerful, motivated, and accomplished.

Do we enjoy it? no ,because we're worrying about it abandoning us. Although we are supposed to be searching for a deeper understanding of things as contemplated through or with time, it should be inspiration to the natural phenomena. "Confucius" states that, the superior man does what is proper to which the state in which he is; he does not desire to go beyond this. "In which we do go beyond the original scope of focus that we started on. So in time there becomes no order, because we contemplate on a mixture of thing and never carry through on one thing. All of us try to order our steps as kings and queen but we never actually put ourselves on that scale. We simply filter the scale to everyone or the people around us.

'Confucius argues that the vicious man is not one who stands at the top of the hierarchy, but one who understands His position in the hierarchy and embraces it to the full. Some people see time as a cage with a one way escape tactic out the same way you came in. Some of the time as a chain gang that guide us to where were supposed to be , to me time is like the one true women that waits for one true love or marriage ; as if she knows it's you. You know through my journey, I have found that time shows us that it's on our side, but we are blinded by our own ambition. We leave time lonely, so when we're doing time it leaves us lonely.

Time prefer strategy sometimes, time conquers states, time leaves a trail of broken hearts, and time has brought the greatest to their knees.

    Contemplated time has created ecstasy when in doubt if there was any, creating loyalist of the broken, move in the state of motion, and accomplished the miserable. "I was ahead of my class as i contemplated life, but I forgot about time that carried life committed its suicide; then time at the brink of death open its eyes, I reconciled, and spoke life to her. Therefore by investing in her life she gave me life. Contemplated I'm understanding now that it's become excellence, my strategy , my love , and my only understanding . Amen...

#12

Exhibit The Part You're Playing

#12

Exhibit The Part You're Playing

Who you are and what you do in the end doesn't come down to a choice; but yet a decision. It is either to be or not to be and until now I have never realized, that really is the question. I have become a man of reason and dominant faith. I am Pimp and therefore I or everyone else will invest in this pimpin. I now understand that it will not be the man who will be challenged; but his teachings. Man I have walked the same as I have walked for years, but that was easy because pettiness was of no importance.

Man, but when you're walking with a reason it's like a ton a bricks added to every step. (Socrates) states that "The life which is unexamined is not worth living." which he also make the good point of, "an unquestioned life is one of ignorance without mortality." And man, that brings us deeper into exhibiting the part you're playing, because when people see you; man they should wonder, think, ponder, or contemplate on what it is like to be you or simply walk in your shoes. If they don't - to me you're in a motion of a purposeless life.

The reason I like Socrates so much for this section, is that he believed that virtue (aret`e in greek , which at that time implied excellence and fulfillment) was " the most valuable of possession." So earlier when I said my "pettiness" I did not mean searching for crumbs, I meant as in skills. Now though I've also possessed skills of obtainment, I didn't know that I lacked the skills of constant elevation. Like most people I found something that I could profit at and used it til the well went dry. Therefore to be excellent and find fulfillment, you must constantly advance, elevate, and conquer every stage of things.

Exhibit the part your playing is more than walking and talking; it's the state of being, even if you're not paying attention or you do things and smile because of who you have become in time and focus on the travel instead of the time traveled. You see this got so deep to me, because I've always had an inquiring mind but I never discovered that thoughts meant a great deal; sense we have so many thoughts per day.

Socrates discovered in a quest to find the wisest men that, "to gain knowledge of the world and oneself it was necessary to realize the limits of one's own ignorance and to remove all preconception. So in exhibiting the part you're playing, I find like Socrates it is not to instruct the people; nor even to simply learn what they know, but to explore the idea they have. I have spent a lot of time exploring the cause I was fighting for, unknowingly throwing away the knowledge I was giving for assumption of ignorance.

"Jalal AD-DIN MUHAMMAD RUMI" (1207 - 1273) ISLAMIC PHILOSOPHER states "don't grieve. Anything you lose comes around in another form. He also quotes, "I died as a mineral and became a plant, I died as plant and rose to animal, I died as an animal and was a man. "So therefore in exhibiting the part I play, I am not tomorrows position, I am todays. So tomorrow I am a movement and exhibiting the part I'm playing cause Pimping to stay in motion and the picture is always seen.

#13

Speech of Pettiness

#13

Speech of Pettiness

One thing that I've heard in the penitentiary is "nigga if you a pimp talk up on a haircut, one of these bitches or even niggas talk up some extra food. First of all nigga that shit was petty, so don't ever disrespect my pimpin again. When you spit, talk on some major shit, and second of all why would I speak up on a haircut when we go to the barber every Wednesday? Why would I talk up on these hoes when the last 10 niggas got caught cause these hoes was scared to lose their job. And why would I be talking on some food when all the meat look like brake pads? People think just cause the pimp has the conversation, he speaks on everything to his advantage.

Some things shouldn't even be on your mind to speak on. Anyways the world is a crazy place, cause if you think about it everybody is trying to talk up on something. You're not supposed to be baptized in ego, but your also not supposed to be to the point where you have no shame in trying to come up on shit that has no importance to your survival. Speaking on petty things is the process of an

unchanging human being. I live the (Heraclitus) philoso-
phy and that is "you can never step in the same river
twice". Which in my situation is that I will never speak of
something that want keep me progressing or evolving. Plus
speaking out of pettiness prevents you from speaking out
of greatness. Pimping speaks when things are out of order,
not just in order to speak. One person that blew my mind
was (Desiderus Erasmus) and he states," to know nothing
is the happiest life."

That made my mouth drop cause petty persons are
satisfied with coming up on nothing. So they are satisfied
with nothing and happy to speak about nothing. So me In
this pimpin I promote, speak only when necessary because
it's not always necessary to speak. So every time I tell
somebody to stop talking for no purpose I'm wasting my
breath, because they are what they are and there's nothing
more to be done. In which in there petty conversations
you can understand that they know there places. So who
am I to help them understand a real niggas position or
stance? In case you come to your senses, "Thinking is not
just something said, but put under consideration before it
becomes verbal.

(Niccolo Machiavelli) states, "The end justifies the means." So if you've spoken a million sermons and the response of your audience seems that you're still a beginner, your means of speaking didn't justify the points end. "The preacher is the main event who speaks out of wisdom and pettiness is the side show there to entertain. Some people listen to me when I speak catchy lyrics from my pimpin, but it seems the minute I start to talking bout education, advancement, the true or even having no time for lollygagging they leave my presence. That's crazy because we have time for pleasure, but no time for the reality of elevating. We have time to speak about nothing ass bitches, but we don't have time to cherish and talk to our wives that as a whole or one you can go many places. Speeches of pettiness excite you tho hun?

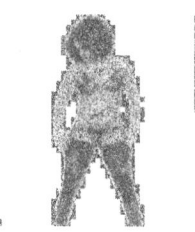

#14

Perfect Everything You Create

#14

Perfect Everything You Create

You see to me it seems impossible to find a Bottom Bitch that defines this *"Hoetation"*. I have searched and search to only find that there will always be a new definition of perfection in every situation. I mean you can get the baddest bitch in the world, but if there is no profit you have lost the biggest war. I mean I've seen go- getters and I have studied their habit but every go-getter doesn't go get it to or of the same degree. So In knowing this I never fell in underestimation when analyzing these hoes. Anyways I've traveled, searched, sought, and wrecked the hoe line to grasp what's mine so we can run this thang.

What does a bitch that can represent you mean? Does it mean for every moment and places. Man I've come across some of the best and worst hoes, serious and silly hoes, meaningless and defined hoes, the most hands off and encumber hoes. Still in all I am still astonished by their audacity to exhibit and promote the position they play and man to me that's deep. Plus I respect these women because even though you are unprofessional, a disgrace, polluted, or your heart, mind, and soul is diseased. They maintain their mentality though and in keeping control of composure you always advance, gain, or rise. In which my point of speaking on this is because, what if my bottom bitch is right at this moment within her advancing stage? What if I'm looking at her in her eyes and dismissed her out of disappointment? Even this bitch is supposed to search and be approved by your pimpin, its strange how your future vision is domino effected by your present disguise.

But understand this though man, when I'm in search for a bottom bitch it only means to the one that fits. You will find a lot of bottom bitches that are extra ordinary and some of the greatest but just because ready, willing, and 100% doesn't make them exact for your pimpin. I made up Hoetation mainly to show the degree of stipulations and qualifications, but just because I said the 50 characteristics of a bottom bitch people think those were the most important characteristics. That doesn't fit everybody though it was just my thoughts on the subject and things change so does people. So my thoughts on it might change, but in building an empire you must hold the highest standards.

In analyzing, searching, and prowling for your bottom bitch that fits you. You must understand that a lot of the times you don't need them to be 100 % when you find them. My favorite motto that I tell these hoes is that, "you don't have to be ready; just be willing. Because one thing in this pimpin is that you gone have to break these hoes down to their basics and in doing so you must build them back up. ***THEREFORE THE END RESULT IS THAT YOU MUST PERFECT EVERYTHING YOU CREATE...*** Therefore a legend or to be left in the history of things you are required not only the pimp but also the "bottom bitch" must always be in search, in look, or in question of.

TO NOT BE IN THAT CONSTANT STATE MEANS YOU ARE AGAINST THE PART YOU PLAY OR THE POSITION YOU STAND. I thought that my nobleness was out of hand but I am not here only for my own ambition, but to create a path for my bottom bitch and my hoe squad to exist in history also. In which if they make it and I don't: I have still made it, because I have ***PERFECTED WHAT I HAVE CREATED AND THE WORLD WILL SEE THEM AS CREA-***

TURES OF MY PERFECTION. Know that majority of the things I write are just my thoughts running rapid, but take me serious because this is my life.

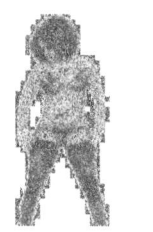

#15

Creation of Prostitution

#15

Creation of Prostitution

Many people look at prostitution as a trade only exampled by women but it is also exampled by men and sad to say but children more and more are included in this. In which back in the days the biggest prostitution was men because slave owners needed their muscle and hard workers. They broke women, men, and children apart for profit; not knowing that this is what denounced their stability. It took away the physical of their strength but gave them mental strength. So in the process of slavery being over (in the history books at least because it still exist) we watched and learned how to sell ourselves and progressed in how to sell others. So we turned it from an oppression to a trademark. Plus along with this trade we innovated.

We brought in trickery , manipulation , the same heartlessness we were given , deception , more flamboyance , the greater lessons , we flip the script from the seller to them being the buyers , we gave it motivation , it inspired us to stand taller , it taught us how to slide between the cracks , walk on egg shells , and promote through our action , etc.........but then for us to prefect or understand something that wasn't for us they provided harsher punishments . So that was the creation of prostitution; through the degrading of a race which to this day is our biggest innovators.

Therefore this is where the modern day pimps came in. You see prostitutes or most of these young hoes that let the world pass them, just didn't have a choice but to let it pass them, or couldn't grasp why it was passing them by. So becoming their end result, they feel they had to catch up in the fast lane and speed off to get where they were supposed to be or beyond.

(I have to still remind you that prostitution was created by the government now they look down on it; just like Pimpin). You see to me prostitution is something of a terroristic bred; they are here to conquer , devour , and leave you to restore the resources .And I love what I do because women are the most dangerous creatures because they can murder with finesse. A man pulls out his penis on some hoes just cause and he is consider a pervert and goes to jail for indecent exposure ,but a women flash the man at McDonalds or puts her pussy out the window at him and she gets a free meal . I'm not complaining, but women complain of how they are treated on a lower level and refuses to use what she got to get what she wants.

Anyways an equation that I live by is loneliness plus manipulation of loneliness equal prostitution. And to me lonely and low are equivalent to each other, because majority of the loneliest people sale themselves in the lowest bids. One of the most popular introductions to prostitution is not just the physical abuse; **though** mainly the mental abuse. People don't understand you see just because you're surrounded by people doesn't mean you're not lonely. Matter of fact those are the loneliest ones and easies targets. In a different sense and on a different higher level, I am lonely because not a lot of people understand my pimp strategies. But from a hoe sense everyone doesn't understand their reasoning or purpose.

In a sense they mostly wonder why they attract the people they are surrounded by and in the same instance they want to understand what set them apart from everyone else. For the simple fact that people are entertained because they merely say nothing and they are only entertained by the effort to comprehend things. Which until they reach the level of knowing who they are and what they represent they will always be unsatisfied.

People think that these hoes are lost but in reality they know how and where they are, though just like pimps we search for only hoes that can fit our pimpin and hoes get exposed. Out of everything that I have seen the craziest things is when these hoes choose niggas that don't know they possess pimpin: but niggas choose hoes that know intention of hoeing and he waste his time trying to convince her. You see hoes actually advance a pimps pimpin, but real pimps show these hoes a brighter light. Beginners get by these hoes because they can't give off perception or walk as if this bitch is telling you something knew. Therefore the next pimp comes along and takes the hoe she want hesitate to leave, because if you can't teach the hoe, you want reach the hoe.

A lot of these hoes search for encumber; which is just someone to take off the burden and she gets that from her pimp. He alleviates her responsibilities in life exchanging for a profitable stability. She see that he handles the stable business effortless, so it becomes pleasing to her to play her part. Therefore in that moment and after this, pimpin becomes what she wants and needs. I now become the crutch to brokenness. Also man, some of these hoes are not searching for stability and love when they prostitute; they use it as their love and stability. So then their end results is justified by the means. For example: A man loves his family and loves going home to his family, but he loves to work on cars deep down in inside. Though it doesn't mean that he has search for love outside of home, but it's what keeps him stable at home.

You see hoes don't neglect positive words, it's just your words has to be relating current and humble to the moment. In which most of these hoes are similar to gravity; they sometimes need a push or pull to cross in, cross out, or cross over. Something simple that everybody fell to see is that, if you upset the established order you will create chaos. So in that chaos you never try to control only persuade this hoes to your convincing direction. So in her eyesight a pimp becomes what she needs not necessarily what she deserves. So you don't question that strategy, it's ok because sometimes it's their faith or mentality stand point that needs to be coerced. So to end this chapter on *"THE CREATION OF PROSTITUTION"*, I leave you with this: The world hammers these hoes to the point of deception they turn to the man/pimp who they don't fully understand.

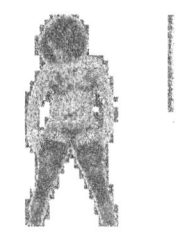

#16

I Wish I Had

#16

I Wish I Had

I wish I had a bitch right now to speak of my intentions. To elaborate my visions to. But what can I say of the bitches who are here? That they are a disgrace that it hurts my heart to see them struggle; but why speak of teaching when regardless they will forever drown. Mainly cause mentality is never their master and matter is of no mind. I wish I could inform every bitch of their ending results without the right navigation but what is her navigation system with no means of transportation.

I asked myself time and time again will I be proud of the legacy that I leave, is it really about the journey, or is this a void movement? I have every bit of faith in the clothe that I'm am breed from , but I refuse to ignore that victory has its sacrifices that even the dedicated sometimes refuse or neglect to promote.

I wish I could allow you to see inside my mentality, take note , and believe this movie in its purest. Fascinated by your own eyes do not block out or regurgitate this foreign message only give permission. Allow me to elevate you from being grounded even though this has grown to become your comfortable state. Allow yourself to live in the bliss and die in certainty. There is no greater love than a pimps love, there is no greater stance than a pimp's corner, and there is no better price to pay.

Forgive me for my arrogance but I am the bread and butter. ***FORGIVE ME FOR THE WAY I WALK BUT LIFE HAS GIVEN ME SO MUCH EXPERIENCE THAT I MUST EXAMPLE ITS OUTCOME.*** What you believe is not important but what you seek is promising. I am not an animal anymore but not because of my age; its cautious patience. How can I teach you without talking? It seems my silence can apprehend the watchful and my words can capture the speechless. Should this remind me of the gift that I am cursed with or does this forget me when or then I'm freed?

I wish I had a bitch that wouldn't daze into wonder when I capture her thoughts, but this is my curse; that I have someone to feel me, instead of praise me. What am I to do with control, when it's all I know? But lift my hands and hope to every now and then bring down chaos. A bitch is my instrument and I am her words. Though I wish I had a bitch to be my words and I be her melody. If I could speak to you the realest shit ever spoke, then I would stand up stomp my feet and dramatize the stage. Remind me when I wake if heaven is reading this and I will rewrite and give it to them explicit as possible; because they can't handle the truth in my words not vulgar but smooth; complicated situation. I wish I had a bitch to speak when spoken to; but instead I hear a mute, which is fine cause your attentive; but hard cause you're in a trance.

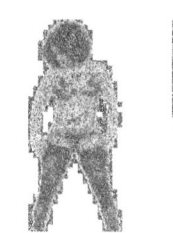

#17

Sensitive and Emotional

#17

Sensitive and Emotional

I came about this chapter because I witnessed a women in the position to neglect. She acted as if I wasn't free and told her to "slide this way cause the sky's this way," that she would rise like yeast and wouldn't fall down as the last crumb. So that brought me to writing this chapter. I wish I had a bitch to talk to, so after writing that chapter; I still couldn't go to sleep because it had taken me to another thought or concept. And it's an attitude that we carry around. Though before I speak on it I want you to know that change has become my doctor intellectually. Anyways man people think that men and women are emotional creatures, but I beg to differ. First understand that this is simply a pimps reflective thinking.

So don't go looking in history, psychology, or statistic books for what I'm saying; this is me analyzing things. I say women are sensitive because if a man she loves has sex with her best friend 7 out of 10 chances are that she'll stop messing with her friend and him, but eventually she return back to him and not the friend. She cry, ask you why and act dramatic; but come back. Mostly cause her brain is sensitive to the male actions. Her brain can live with and except what love acknowledge as strength to her. Therefore she can hold and take in more. Giving her power that she actually doesn't know she possess.

On the other hand the man is emotional and I say that because in the same scenario; if she has sex with his best friend, she a slut or a bitch. And in truth he would accept her back but his emotions carry a picture that has never before been seen and he can't shake it (another man between her legs). So he acts out of emotions and his brain hardens to that fact. So his brain can never eliminate what's needed to revive love lost, only except love that was lost or what love has done. So he acts out of emotion and says I slept with her, her, and her. And she takes to the grave the person other than what she told; the him, him, and him that she has slept with.

Meanwhile making you feel bad for your and her wrong doings. Men are emotional to the fact that someone has penetrated the womb that he claims. Women are sensitive because you have the audacity to think you played her and it hurts not because of what you have done, but because you tried to play her in an abusive way. Men believe that wounds will heal over the emotional times spent. Women believe that time will heal the wounds of her sensitivity. Therefore women become sensitive by sight and men become emotional by mentality. Which is why you trick or spend money on them because of the illusion it presents. And the reason why you give in because of the movie that plays in your head.

SENSITIVE AND EMOTIONAL

PART 2

Spaghetti & Banana Effect

1. When you apply pressure or heat to anything it hardens or softens. (Therefore a woman's heart is hard becoming soft and the man is soft becoming hard.)

2. A woman's brain let sensitivity of the situation seeps through her brain

3. A man's brain let the emotions of the situation play like a movie in the brain caging emotions to replay hardening a selfish heart.

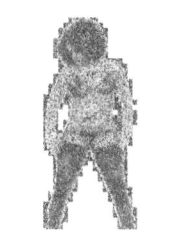

#18

I Had A Dream

#18

I Had A Dream

The other night I had a dream, that I returned to the same cell that held me hostage for so long and then I woke up. So I asked the lord to help me make sense of this and to my demise no answer came. So I simply figured at some point I was destined to return to this hell hole. So now today I had similar dream that I was playing a game or in a game then all of a sudden the guard came to lock me up in a room with bars , Saying he would be back to let me out. Well time passed and passed; no guard. ***By the way my family was trapped with me***, so it seemed like a friendly game. So the first person I could see or hear I told them that I had been here so long that the guard was supposed to be coming back a long time ago and the faces that responded looked familiar.

In which he said you have the rest of the day to finish the game and I say you know me, turned around and understood that I knew how to get out. Meanwhile the guard looked at me rolled his eyes and locked me in with my own satisfaction. So I began to push certain bricks in on the wall as if it was some kind of puzzle. And one side of the wall opened and here was nothing there but empty bunks, spider webs, and ancient ghost of memory. So I told my family to go first because I solved the puzzle.

As man I am sacrifice to my family. Though I didn't get to finish, I woke up with understanding. I figured out the game. I was so in a rush to get back to streets and succeed that I didn't understand that I can still succeed and come back to this hell and even though I'm rich and successful; that doesn't separate me from the rest that are here because I am still left In the footsteps of the man who didn't take heed to his dream. I still remain blind to the fact and left to continuously play the game until it ends you with life or death. Some fun game hun? Thank God for understanding. Guide my path please and take these broken wings! I was spending time showing my people the adventures of the life I was living; that it drowned all of us.

#19

CHANGE

#19

CHANGE

A word so simple; yet so complex but gives reason and glorifies experience. If words are the preacher and living is the sermon, therefore change is not the product of the audience ; but the deacons . You see today's eyes consist of trend and trend provides the heart with no intentions to change and lead only to follow. We can graduate from the hood and the streets, but we fail to graduate from its presence. Change is deeper than moving on; it is the art of taking on a different rode. I can't stop drowning from my wrongs unless I start swimming toward my rights. Change is so hard for so many because it puts you in the position to advance out of and into.

Therefore advancing means or gives opportunity with no choice but to push, cry, and bleed out of misery and weakness to keep in the strength and ambition. Whoever knew that 6 letters could hurt so badly? Everyone. That is why change is uncommon are should I say faceless. I can give in to fate or I can breathe out to having faith in the things that can birth change. For a wise man can only be wise when his feet are planted, but ignorance will always be ignorance because it will never find or seek a point of stability. (PIMP_SUASION) To me the letters in change stand for : (choose how abusive nature guarantees existence) an that's because people that say I'll change tomorrow abusing resources of evolving and finally when to old they realize existence isn't guaranteed. So to the wine-oes I will become "the good to the last drop" because they refuse to stop killing themselves.

To the drug dealer I will become the "A1 DROP" because they refuse to stop living under the street lights. To the people who will keep the same routine until the day they die " I will become the most seductive rodes, because I know how and where you stand . In which we all beg people to change, but change is not where you're going. It's the position you play and all some can do is participate in their position; while others break barriers out of that position .My mind has become of a God 'My thoughts of sky with no clouds; my heart as beautiful as the blue sea, the one thing change and life has in common is life has no emotions and no favorites. So I must manipulate what I see as I see. Therefore in my changing, limitless options breeds difficulty in the definition of righteous.

#20

Quest To Unite

#20

Quest To Unite

I was just sitting around thinking about if I had someone to cherish or express thoughts to and what would I say? So here it is. I thought of you and I smiled, I thought of us and damn near couldn't keep the strength to stand. At times these thoughts make me contemplate what I require from, out, and within a women but then emotions have to take over.

When I was a child I brushed it aside as a silly game, but now that I am a man I can only ask for what a man should want. and that is you. Though the strangest conclusion come at awkward times , the most important thing I would rather know is how do or did I come to this result. Then it came to me that I am a gentlemen and have no choice but to require the best. So does that make you the best? Only if we agree to agree. I have been waiting so hard and long for heaven to send an angel right here on earth. Meanwhile you had every intention to vacuum a Don up in your heaven. Why does the words I speak or whisper to you seem like lyrics of ecstasy? I would ask for a chance to have to hold, for richer, or for poorer until death do us part, but what is the chance of producing two of the greatest that ever did it.

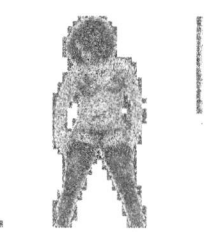

#21

A Better Author

#21

A Better Author

Inaugurate my presence as if life won't allow me into its office. Embrace my courage to carry on though I'm not as strong as I seem. Decipher my meaning so my burners are not my downfall. I feel as if this marathon will never be over. Obedient is not my absence but my fault and honor has not my love but my pain. Negativity has shined his light of reflection. So it is possible to grow. Does this make me a scholar; a learned person, a reflective thinker, because my pass has become this effort of advancement.

Separation has added a greater scenario to my scheme. Qualification seems to not matter in a world of trends. At times I feel I'm a nuclear reactor about to melt down but this seems not to be my story. At times I feel like a great American song bird that refuses to listen stuck in my own category. In a world of eat or be eating I feel like I should be a cannibal because the world is facing me growling. This is the confession of a better author.

I'm not considerate of the inside box , but a psycho of the unseen limits. I did not learn from public school but learned from being of the public schools. What is the potential difference; that one covered me and the other one left me exposed? I don't feel as if a conversation, but that I stand in this mist of an orientation. I choose not to imitate my struggle, but to innovate my character. Am I a great author? No… a better author because some of the greatest legacy's will go unlived until the day of death. I am not superior to time but I will be to the past.

When you see a
Bad BITCH on the BLOCC

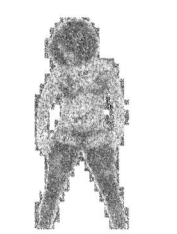

#22

Convert

#22

Convert

Knowledge is not just the art of ***"KNOWING THE LEDGE"*** to me, but the art of being able to comprehend how to become the roots of a tree that can create branches of or in your own. You see obtaining knowledge allows you to be able to convert, manipulate, or disarm even the sharpest brain. Do you understand what I mean by the sharpest brain? That there are people on point in more than one subject, but to obtain knowledge; is to be well rounded 360.

Though my guess of where knowledge started was as a marathon for and of self but ended up exposing the very grave simplicity of the world's ability to maintain the conversation I carry therein. To get off the subject for just 5 seconds to allow you to see or observe my greatest visions, hopes, and expectations; is that my children appreciate the effects of growing in knowledge and that I find a way that we can relate it to not only their life, but their pleasures. Knowing that something or somehow has allow me to respond so prominent to the casualties of my duties or occupation as if it has become my code not of silence or speech; but of action. In which it seems to me now I have sponged up so much my thoughts should be researched and analyzed. Then I ran across a man one day with all intentions to convert and then I began to look at my own means.

You see his purpose was for means of religious beliefs and mine is for religion of pimpin. Therefore he spoke everywhere he goes and I speak only where required or appropriate. In which is the reason why I learned or better yet how I learned to exceed my own boundaries, because you must reach the moment where knowledge elevates you to the point where time, life, and space is just simply too small to contain your not only speech but one word. Also I have to remember that in the moment I participate in; is that game or knowledge is to be sold to the loyal bidder. No one knows but at times I cry out to knowledge in thanks that at the ending of the day, I am left standing in a river bed of books wrapped around a cage in my own head.

In return I find myself converting so many people from what I'm thinking in my brain to seeing my thoughts as passion to people. But how did I create this? Is it my speech? Must I stop talking? Because if I don't my every word will give insight to knowledge, though that is not my intentions because to me this seems to be a simple conversation. So does "conversation" actually mean "convert sensation" of the brain. Though I would hate to be cloned if this means advancement to "us" as a whole; I am sacrifice...

#23

Thinking of Home

#23

Thinking of Home

Heavenly father forgive me of my sins. As I look through the clouds I drift into a daze. Sometimes my tears live freely on my face as a bum under the bridge. Therefore these thoughts lead me to reflection of self. My heartlessness has completely taken me over and I wonder that even if I love my children, will they feel that same passion and will it take them over too. I try so hard to bring precision to the purpose but it continuously flip and have fun with me as a little kid jumping on a mattress in the projects. My mind has become so engaged that not only my physical but my mental has its up and downs combining 10 roller coasters.

I'm hoping that Jesus rescues me because of my faith. I'm standing because Jesus got my back because of my humbleness, but deep down inside me I'm shivering with uncertainty because it's what has given me my major setbacks . My test has been trial and error, but elevation has made my soul either weak or strong. In which my mentality is stronger and stronger every day, though no-

body would admit it the mind wears and tares sometimes .This leaves the heart in place of the banana in the
tail pipe. My mother told me that the sun will shine soon
and now I see it and it feels beautiful on my skin, but does
Jesus agree with the deep feeling or has so much time to
think suddenly became a deep burden of mine.

Some would say that prison keeps a daddy from
being a father; and well it does; because I don't know
about anyone else but I can't wait to be a father for my
kids. To teach them, raise them, hold them, secure them,
and love and nature them, so that these broken wings never becomes a cycle. In Jesus name here my prayers I'm
close to giving up not on you but my destiny because it has
left me eager and unable to sleep. There is none deserving
in my eyes. Though I know I'm at the finish line waiting
for you to give me permission to cross, it seems the devil
has strapped to me and left me confused and you're just
waiting to see what I would do. Congratulations to me!!!
I'm crossing the finish line no more "thinking of home".
Now I'm "home thinking" that "I" was the hold up!!! I'm
ready A-men.

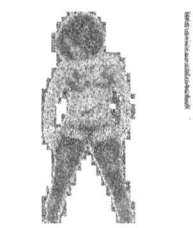

#24

Pimp Cardio

#24

Pimp Cardio

This section is more of helping a pimp know of the people he come in contact, communicating, or socializing with. Coming in grips with people every day and being so immune of our own conversation; we began to talk to everyone the same, except with a different gestures. Though it seems harmless, the problem with that is just this; people love our conversation but don't get our conversation; people hear our conversation but never listen to our words; or while people are exposed to our conversation they never take advantage of the knowledge it gives. Which is why you have to work it out of them, giving the title to this section" Pimp Cardio".

First, know how you stand as a teacher and that every uneducated learner will not be a student in your class. Especially cause every hoe doesn't fit your pimpin and there are very few niggas who deserve the game. Second, this pertains to the physical, not only mental, because a pimp moves in the mental but maneuvers in the physical. Therefore your physical attributes will sometimes be what

completely marry a bitch over to you. Third you must always be able to move a hoe physically and mentally sta-
tioning her pockets, but know that hoes come and go. In
which an un-stabilized hoe "in" your pimpin, will guaran-
tee profit and elevation "to" your status. Fourth teach a
hoe to be a bitch, because just cause she has a pussy
doesn't mean she was taught to carry a pussy. Most of
these hoes got bigger dicks then niggas, though not only
that, man a hoe searches for direction or leadership because she's never seen it in the terms of her choice of living. Fifth teach her your expectations, because even
though you reiterate plans, commands, or duties that
doesn't direct itself.

Thoughts are great but to be taught another's
thoughts, plans commands, or duty's is gratifying. Sixth
teach her the world around her, this will make her comfortable in getting or receiving not only the things she
need, but the things she want. Also this allows her to question the things, people, and world around her with a sense
of security, while their starring faces are ready to question.
Seventh then you teach her to walk confident in the worlds
she will have to enter. It will show and tell her how to
adapt to her environment and be productive. Eight teach

her how to motivate stars to only shine in her presence. She will pay for it, but you must guide her on how to make people tick till she say tock.

This will be your long time profit assurance. Ninth supply moments for her to cherish. In order for her to enjoy victory of the goals you set and taste that joy, you must supply those moments from jump start. Meanwhile coming from your visions she will live and die how you seem fit physically and mentally. Tenth and last but not least, the sole purpose of this brief pimp cardio is that you can have a hoe or student and raise them on your pimpin, but in the long run if not taught this in many correct forms, this will only persuade people of the knowledge not their actions. "Because it is better to grip a thing whole heartedly than to be in or of that thing short lived". (Pimp Suasion).

Thank You for Your support.

-The Priest-

About the Author

Pimp Suasion ' The Priest', born Tommy Chatman in Lake Charles, Louisiana. He graduated from Lagrange High School. His love for writing and curiosity came from high school English and History classes. He has a passion for searching for more than the written truth nurtured him. Although never attending college he educated himself about the world around him and also outside the box of that world. The father of three children Zephenia, Tarig and Adolph born to Jonnie Chatman and Tommy Galmore. He was the oldest of three, Brady and Eric Chatman. He is also an artist, songwriter and motivational speaker. This book is not only about Pimpin and Streets but to understand our position in life period. In which Rules and Regulations have been cast out to the seas of forgetfulness. This book is about Curiosity and Overcoming.

Presenting: "The White Dwarf"

To Contact and For Booking:

tps944@yahoo.com

facebook.com/tommy.chatman.127

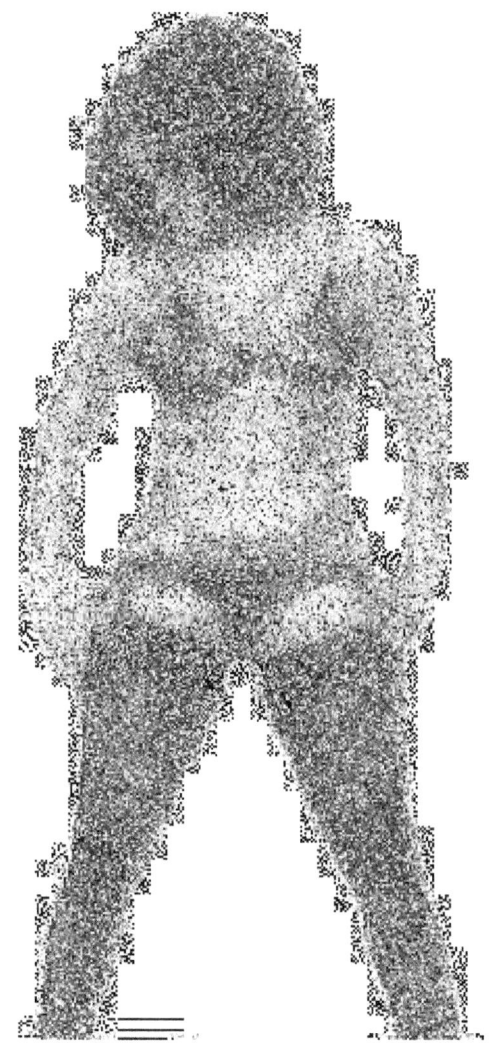

www.ingramcontent.com/pod-product-compliance
Lightning Source LLC
Chambersburg PA
CBHW071127250626
47159CB00006B/2160